Letterland

Bedtime Stories

Selected and edited by
Louis Fidge

Contents

Collins Educational
An imprint of HarperCollins*Publishers*

Illustrations

David Eaton

Clever Cat's Café
The Trouble with Telephones
Naughty Nick's Good Day

Anna Jupp

Hairy Hat Man's Hiccups
Bouncy Ben and the Bubble
Robber Red meets Santa Claus
Kicking King and the Kittens

Jan West (colouring by Gina Hart)

Zig Zag Zebra comes to Letterland
Golden Girl and the Garden Party
A New Job for Lucy

Published by Collins Educational
An imprint of HarperCollins*Publishers* Ltd
77-85 Fulham Palace Road
London W6 8JB

© Lyn Wendon 1997

First published 1997

ISBN 0 00 303366 X

LETTERLAND® is a registered trademark of Lyn Wendon.

British Library Cataloguing in Publication Data
A catalogue record for this book is available from the British Library.

Printed by Scotprint Ltd, Musselburgh

Hairy Hat Man's Hiccups

by Emma Duncan

...sixty, sixty-one...

Hairy Hat Man had a new friend. Humphrey the Hippo was visiting Letterland for his half-term holiday.

Hairy Hat Man and Humphrey decided to have a game of Hide and Seek. Humphrey counted to a hundred while Hairy Hat Man hid.

"One hundred! Coming, ready or not!" hollered Humphrey.

He couldn't see Hairy Hat Man anywhere, but then he heard a strange sound.

"Hic . . . hic . . . hic . . ."

Humphrey followed the sound, and there hiding behind a hedge was . . .

. . . Hairy Hat Man.

"Oh dear," said Hairy Hat Man sadly. "I've got hiccups. We can't really play Hide and Seek until they go away, or you'll find me every time."

"Well then, we'll just have to get rid of them," said Humphrey the Hippo.

"How?" asked Hairy Hat Man.

Then he had an idea. "I know. Let's go and ask Clever Cat. She's very clever. She'll know what to do."

"I do hope so," said Humphrey, glumly. He wanted to play Hide and Seek.

Clever Cat was very helpful. "Have you tried doing a headstand?" she asked.

"What a good idea," said Humphrey hopefully.

But Hairy Hat Man looked sad.

"I can do *hand*stands," he said, "but I can't stand on my *head*. It would squash my hairy hat!"

So Hairy Hat Man and Humphrey decided to ask Ticking Tess if she had any ideas.

Ticking Tess looked puzzled.

"How about hopping?" she suggested.

Hairy Hat Man looked hopeful.
He was good at hopping and his hat wouldn't get squashed.

He started hopping up and down.
Hop, hop, hop, hop, hop, hop.

He huffed and puffed . . . and then he hiccupped again.

"Huh! It's not working, and I've been hopping for hic . . . half an hour, sighed Hairy Hat Man. "I'm getting fed up with these hic . . . hiccups."

"Me too," said Humphrey. "I really want to play Hide and Seek."

"We might have to play Hopscotch instead," said Hairy Hat Man sadly. "Wait, I have one more idea. Let's ask Naughty Nick."

Now Naughty Nick is a very noisy boy, and noise is the one thing that Hairy Hat Man hates. So he doesn't go near Naughty Nick very often. But everyone knew that Nick often had good ideas for solving problems.

A lot of noise was coming from Naughty Nick's workshop.

"Oh help!" said Hairy Hat Man. "All this hullabaloo is just too much. It's giving me a headache. Hic . . . We'll just have to go home and play Hopscotch instead."

Humphrey wasn't very happy, but they both began the long hike back to Hairy Hat Man's house.

"My feet hurt, and I'm hungry," said Humphrey. "Do you think we could have a rest?"

"Good idea, Humphrey," said Hairy Hat Man. "These hic . . . hiccups are making me quite tired."

Humphrey sat down on a hummock, and so did Hairy Hat Man. But no sooner had Hairy Hat Man sat down than he jumped up again with a howl.

"Heeouch!" he howled.

Humphrey nearly jumped out of his skin. He had never heard Hairy Hat Man make so much noise. Something must be horribly wrong.

"I've sat on something sharp," whispered Hairy Hat Man.

They both turned round to see what Hairy Hat Man had sat on. Two beady eyes stared back up at them.

"What is it?" asked Humphrey.

"My name's Helen. I'm a hedgehog," said a grumpy voice.

"You're very sharp," said Hairy Hat Man.

"Well that's so people don't sit on me," muttered Helen.

"I'm so sorry," said Hairy Hat Man. "I promise I won't do it again."

Suddenly, Humphrey noticed something.

"Hey! Hairy Hat Man! Guess what?" cried Humphrey. "Your hiccups have gone!"

Hairy Hat Man was quiet for a moment. Then he laughed.

"Ho ho! You're right, Humphrey. Hip, hip, hooray!"

"Glad to be helpful," grinned Helen, "even though you did bend a few of my spines."

The three of them decided to play Hide and Seek together.

"One, two . . . one hundred, coming ready or not," cried Helen, and she scampered happily off to look for Humphrey and Hairy Hat Man.

Zig Zag Zebra comes to Letterland

by Julie McLaren and Jo Hallett

This story happened long, long ago, when the alphabet was a little shorter than it is now.

One day, Bouncy Ben came bouncing out of his burrow as usual – and nearly jumped out of his skin. There, lying under a tree by the side of the river, was a strange black and white animal. It was fast asleep and making a funny little snoring noise, like this: Zzzz, Zzzz, Zzzz.

Bouncy Ben tiptoed slowly up to the creature. He was very, very quiet, but it woke up with a jump and galloped away so fast it was gone before he could blink.

A little later, Dippy Duck was shaking herself to get her feathers dry, when something zipped past her so fast that she fell back into the water with a splash.

"What was that?" she wondered.
But it had gone so quickly she couldn't really see.

Meanwhile, Jumping Jim was jumping happily along towards his jigsaw house. It had been raining and there were lots of puddles in the road, so he had to jump very carefully. Suddenly, something black and white whizzed past him so fast that he jumped the wrong way and landed right in a puddle.

"That's the first time I've ever jumped straight into a puddle," he said to himself. "How on earth did that happen?"

Before long, nearly everyone in Letterland had seen something black and white zoom past them in a blur.

Some of them thought it was a horse.

"Perhaps someone has been painting it!" suggested Sammy Snake – but his sister Sally Snake said, "That's sssilly.

"I know," said Fireman Fred, "I'll squirt foam on it next time it comes by. That should stop it running round Letterland knocking everyone over."

So Fireman Fred got his hose, and hid behind the fence in front of Jumping Jim's garden. The others looked out of the windows in Jumping Jim's jigsaw house to see what would happen next.

It wasn't long before they heard the sound of galloping hooves again. Fireman Fred shot foam into the middle of the road. But he was too late. There was a quick black and white flash and the creature had gone.

The foam missed it, and instead hit Robber Red, who was walking down the road minding his own business for once. Suddenly he was no longer red, but white all over!

"Help, a snowstorm!" cried Robber Red, trying to see through all the foam.

"That's no sssnowstorm," hissed Sammy Snake. "No, it's a fffoamstorm," added Fireman Fred, "and it was meant to catch a strange black and white creature, not a red one!"

"Now what's all this fuss about?" asked Clever Cat, yawning and stretching as she came along to see who was making all the noise. She had been asleep most of the afternoon, and hadn't seen the strange black and white creature.

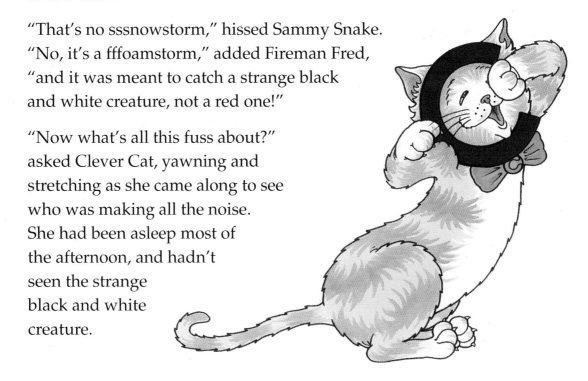

"There's a funny black and white animal running around very fast, and knocking us over," said Dippy Duck.

"Sssomeone's been painting it!" hissed Sammy Snake.

"Wait a minute," said Clever Cat, who was wide awake by now. "It sounds like a zebra to me. I don't think it meant to knock you over. It's probably just frightened."

"Fireman Fred tried to put foam on it," said Ticking Tess.

"Well that won't help," said Clever Cat. "We must show it we are friends." She sent everyone back into their houses and put some hay and sugar lumps in the middle of the road.

After a while, the zebra came by again. This time, it stopped to eat the food. It looked very tired. Clever Cat went up to it slowly, and soon they were talking together.

Gradually, all the other Letterland people and animals came and gathered around Clever Cat and the zebra.

"Her name is Zig Zag Zebra and she was only whizzing everywhere because she was lost and frightened," Clever Cat told them. "She comes from a land far away and her home was destroyed by a forest fire."

Very gently, they led Zig Zag Zebra to the Letterland Zoo and introduced her to Zak the Zoo Keeper. Zak thought she was beautiful, and he asked her if she would like to be his very special pet at the Zoo.

Zig Zag Zebra was too shy to say anything, but at least she wasn't frightened any more. She managed to smile at Zak, who stroked her neck and led her to a pile of sweet straw so that she could have a rest. Zig Zag Zebra was so tired that she fell asleep straight away.

That night, everyone could hear the gentle snoring sounds of the sleeping zebra.

"Zzzz Zzzz Zzzz."

The next day, Zak and all the others made Zig Zag Zebra feel so welcome that she said shyly that she would like to stay. And she has lived in Letterland ever since!

14

Clever Cat's Café

by Pauliina Malinen

Clever Cat was very excited. Her cousin Carol had invited her to stay for a few days' holiday. Carol lived in a little cottage in the country.

But although Clever Cat was excited, she was also rather worried.

Eddy Elephant noticed that Clever Cat was not quite herself. "What's wrong, Clever Cat?" he asked.

"My cousin Carol has invited me to stay," explained Clever Cat. "I'd love to go, but I'd have to close my café if I do." She had only recently opened her café and she had lots of customers who came every day for a cup of coffee and some cake.

"But that's no problem at all!" exclaimed Eddy Elephant. "I'll gladly look after the café while you're gone. I'm sure Jumping Jim and Munching Mike would love to help, too."

Clever Cat's face lit up. "Really?" she cried, smiling from ear to ear.

So it was all arranged. As soon as Clever Cat had left, Eddy Elephant took over the café, with the help of Jumping Jim and Munching Mike.

"This is mmmarvellous!" said Munching Mike, dropping some meringues and a few slices of melon on the floor in his excitement.

Jumping Jim began juggling with some jellies. While he juggled, he jumped up and down around the café. Now, although Jumping Jim is a brilliant juggler, the jellies began to slip off their plates. Suddenly, he couldn't catch them any more and all four slippery pink jellies landed – splat, splat, splat, splat – on the floor.

Eddy Elephant started to look very worried about the state of the café, but he didn't have time to say anything to the others because the first customer had just come through the door.

It was Quarrelsome Queen.

"Good morning, Your Majesty!" gasped Eddy Elephant. "What would you like for breakfast?" "I want Clever Cat's special coffee and cream cake. I can't start my day without them," snapped Quarrelsome Queen.

"Clever Cat has gone away for a couple of days. I don't know how to make her cream cake, but what about some of my special scrambled eggs? They're jolly tasty," suggested Eddy Elephant.

"All right then," said Quarrelsome Queen, "but be quick. I'm in a hurry!"

Eddy started to make the scrambled eggs as fast as he could. But he felt enormous in the tiny kitchen, and he ended up knocking lots of things on to the floor by accident. He even dropped the egg he was holding in his trunk. And on top of everything else, a long queue had started to form behind Quarrelsome Queen.

Quarrelsome Queen finally lost her patience. "Enough! I can't wait any longer. I'm off to the castle!" And she swept out of the café.

17

Eddy Elephant sighed sadly and turned to the next customer.
It was Sammy Snake.

"Good to sssee you, Eddy," he hissed. "I'd just like to have a cup of
tea with some sugar, please."

Eddy sighed with relief. This was going to be easier! He turned
towards Munching Mike. "Would you please get Sammy Snake a
nice cup of tea?" he asked.

Munching Mike was chewing on something and he quickly gulped it
down. Then he looked at Eddy and said in a guilty voice, "I'm afraid
we've just run out of tea spoons . . .".

Eddy guessed straight away what had happened. He knew how much
his metal monster friend loved to eat anything made of metal.
Munching Mike had eaten all the spoons!

Luckily, Sammy Snake knew all about Munching Mike and he wasn't
angry. "Never mind," he said, "I'll stir my tea with my tail instead."

Eddy was getting very upset by now. He had wanted to enjoy himself, but everything was going wrong! What was Clever Cat going to say when she came back?

"Clever Cat trusted us with the café and we've ruined everything," he sobbed. He sat down on the steps outside the café and wished that he had never offered to help Clever Cat. There were no customers coming in any more, because everybody had heard about the muddle and the mess.

After a while, however, Eddy Elephant noticed two more customers coming towards the café. His heart sank when he realised they were Clever Cat and her cousin Carol.

"Hello, Eddy," called Clever Cat cheerfully. "I've come back early because my cousin Carol wanted to come and see my café. How is it going?"

Eddy buried his head between his enormous feet and mumbled, "See for yourself . . ."

So the cousins went inside the café and Eddy waited unhappily outside.

After a while, Clever Cat and her cousin came out again, smiling happily, and asked Eddy to join them for a cup of coffee.

Eddy was very puzzled. He went into the café and looked around.

To his amazement, everywhere was clean and tidy. The café positively sparkled, and there was a delicious smell of apple tarts coming from the oven. Munching Mike and Jumping Jim were chatting to Ticking Tess and Ticking Tom.

"Thank you! Thank you!" whispered Eddy Elephant.

Munching Mike and Jumping Jim explained. "We tried to clean the place up, but we couldn't have done it without the help of Ticking Tess and Ticking Tom. We telephoned them and they came straight away and started tidying up."

Eddy Elephant smiled an enormous smile. Then they all sat down together and ate apple tarts.

Slowly, customers started to return and Clever Cat offered them all coffee and cream cakes. Everyone had such a nice time that they didn't even think of complaining that they didn't have any spoons!

Bouncy Ben and the Bubble

by Susan Welby

"Bother! Bother! Bother!" shouted Bouncy Ben, as he bounced upstairs to his bedroom. Ben is usually a bright and cheerful bunny, but today he was in a very bad mood.

"But *I'm* the best! I'm best at everything!" he shouted, bouncing crossly on his bed.

"Ben, be careful! You'll break the bed," said his mother, who had come upstairs to see what all the banging was about.

"But I'm the best at balancing a ball between my ears! I can burrow faster and deeper than any rabbit in Letterland, and no-one is better at bouncing balloons!" boasted Ben.

"Well, you've certainly got the biggest head in Letterland," said his Mum. "Why don't you go outside and play Bunny Bounce with your brothers?"

"I don't want to because, just now, I saw Billy bounce higher than any rabbit has ever bounced before. He's my baby brother and he's already a better bouncer than I'll ever be!" blurted Ben.

"Well, we can't all be best at everything," said his Mum. "I'll run you a nice warm bath. That'll make you feel much better."

Later, as Ben lay back in the bath, he had a brilliant idea. "Billy got a brand new bottle of bubble bath for his birthday," he thought. And he emptied the whole bottle into the bath. "Serves him right for being a better bouncer than me!"

Ben soon began to feel better. He splashed about until the bath brimmed with big bright bubbles. Then he blew and blew and blew . . .

. . . and the bubbles grew bigger and bigger and bigger.

In the end, the biggest bubble Ben had ever seen bobbed right up out of the water and floated up into the air. It nearly filled the bathroom.

"I've got to show this to someone," thought Ben. "This must be the biggest, the brightest, the very best bubble anyone has ever blown!"

Very, very gently, Ben stretched his arms around the bubble and caught it. The bubble began to bounce up and down, but Ben held on. Slowly, it bounced towards the open window, but still Ben didn't let go . . .

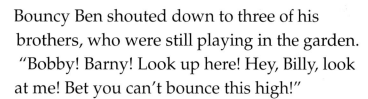

Then the bubble squeezed through the window and Ben *still* wouldn't let go. Now the bubble was bobbing through the sky and Ben *couldn't* let go!

Bouncy Ben shouted down to three of his brothers, who were still playing in the garden. "Bobby! Barny! Look up here! Hey, Billy, look at me! Bet you can't bounce this high!"

But Ben's brothers didn't look up, because they couldn't hear him.

Ben and the bubble went on bobbing up and up and up. "Look at me! I'm high in the sky! Hey, Clever Cat, can you see? Can't catch me! I'm bouncing higher than anyone has ever bounced before!"

But Clever Cat didn't look up, because she couldn't hear him.

As Ben and the bubble rose higher and higher over Letterland, Ben shouted louder and louder. "Look at me! I've blown the biggest bubble anyone has ever blown and I'm bouncing it!"

But no-one looked up, because no-one could hear him.

Then the bubble bounced into a cloud. The cloud puffed open and Ben was sucked inside. The cloud was soft and warm, but Ben couldn't see his friends any more.

He began to feel very lonely and not very brave at all. "If only I hadn't used all Billy's bubble bath, this wouldn't have happened," he thought sadly. "If only I hadn't been so bothered about being the best at everything . . ."

Suddenly, the cloud blew open. Ben and the bubble floated out into the sky again, but now a breeze was blowing them towards a tree. "Be careful, bubble!" shouted Ben.

First there was a BUMP, then a very loud BANG. The bubble burst – and Ben was left dangling from a branch. "Help!" he yelled. "I'm stuck!"

Ben wondered if he could bounce down from the branch. But it was too far. He looked down. Far below was a prickly blackberry bush. "I'm bound to fall straight into those brambles," he thought.

Just then, Ben heard a voice. "Hey, Ben! Down here!" Ben turned his head and looked down. Billy, Bobby and Barny were on the ground calling up to him.

"I'm stuck!" called Ben. "Can you help me down?"

His brothers had an idea. Bobby stretched up and hugged the tree trunk. Barny clambered up and stood on Bobby's head. Billy bounced up and balanced on Barny's head.

Then Billy shouted, "Bounce on to my back, Ben!"

So Ben bounced on to Billy's back. Then Billy and Ben bounced down Barny and Bobby . . .

. . . and in no time at all, all four brothers had bounced back down on to the ground again.

"Ooh, you're so brave, Ben!" cried Billy. "Fancy bouncing up into that tree. You really are the best bouncer in Letterland after all."

But Ben wasn't going to boast about something he hadn't done. "I didn't *bounce* into that tree," he explained. "I *bumped* into it." And Ben told his brothers the whole story, including the bit about using up all Billy's bubble bath.

"I'm sorry, Billy. I blamed you for being a better bouncer than I am," he said. "If I hadn't been so bothered about being the best, none of this would have happened."

Luckily, Billy didn't mind at all. "Well, if you didn't bounce up into that tree, I must still be the best bouncer in Letterland," he shouted, and he bounced off to tell everyone.

That night, Ben lay in his bed, thinking about his big adventure with the bubble.

"Billy is the best bouncer in Letterland," he thought, "but I don't mind. I'm the *luckiest* bouncer in Letterland. I blew the biggest, the brightest, the very best bubble anyone ever saw . . .

. . . except no-one actually saw it . . ."

And Ben drifted gently off to sleep.

Golden Girl and the Garden Party

by Katie Carr

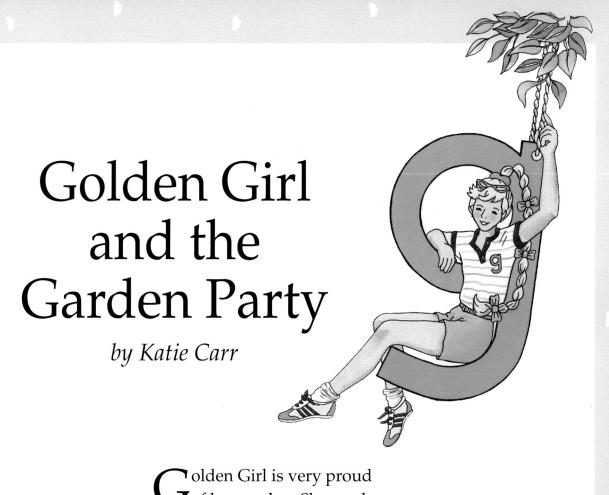

Golden Girl is very proud of her garden. She works hard to keep the weeds away so that all kinds of beautiful flowers can grow – primroses and daffodils in the Spring, roses and sunflowers and gladioli in the Summer, and so many other flowers that not even Clever Cat can name them all!

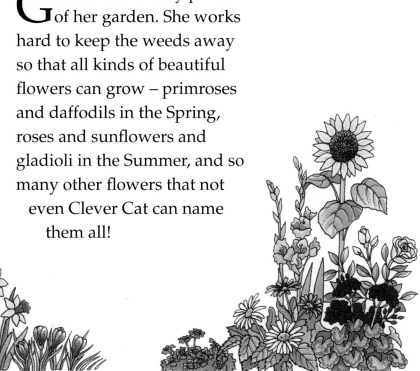

Even in the Winter, when most of the garden is asleep under a blanket of snow, Golden Girl is sure to be in her warm greenhouse, planting new seeds ready for next year.

When all her work is done, Golden Girl loves to sit on her garden swing and sway gently in the breeze. And that was just where Jumping Jim expected to find her when he jumped into the garden one afternoon in late Spring. It had been a beautiful day and he had seen Golden Girl earlier, pushing her wheelbarrow across her garden.

"She must be tired after working so hard on such a warm day," said Jumping Jim to himself. But he could see straight away that Golden Girl wasn't on her swing. Instead, she was kneeling down beside one of the flower beds, and she seemed to be looking for something.

"Oh, Jim!" she cried when she saw Jumping Jim, and she ran to meet him. "Can you help me, please?"

"Whatever is the matter?" asked Jumping Jim. "Have you lost something?"

Golden Girl burst into tears.

"I've lost my little golden goose," she sobbed. "It was on my golden chain, and it was a special gift from my Mum and Dad. They'll be so upset when I tell them."

"Now, don't worry," said Jumping Jim in a soothing voice. "If you've lost your golden goose in the garden, I'm sure we'll be able to find it again."

He jumped high over the garden so that he could see over the flower beds and hedges more easily.

"Can you see it?" called Golden Girl anxiously.

"No, I'm afraid I can't," said Jumping Jim sadly. "I think it's too small for me to see from the sky. We'll just have to search every corner of the garden."

The two of them searched carefully until the sun started to go down and the garden became dark and shadowy. But there was no sign of the little golden goose on its golden chain.

Golden Girl turned sadly to her friend.

"Thank you for trying to help me," she said with a sigh, "but it's no use. I don't know what I shall do . . . "

"Just a minute, Golden Girl," said Jumping Jim. "I think I've got an idea. I've thought of a way for you to earn some money. Then you'll be able to buy a new golden goose and golden chain! You must hold a Garden Party, and everyone will pay to come in and enjoy your garden. You can even sell some flowers and some little plants, too!"

Golden Girl clapped her hands in delight.

"What a wonderful idea!" she cried. "I've just started growing some seedlings in my greenhouse – I can sell all the extra ones. I'll make some cakes, too, and all my visitors can sit in the garden to have their tea!"

So Golden Girl was even busier than usual for the next few days. She made the garden neat and tidy, and borrowed some tables and chairs from her friends.

Impy Ink drew some posters to tell everyone about the Garden Party, and Jumping Jim jumped all over Letterland putting up the posters where people would be sure to see them.

LETTERLAND FRIENDS!
PLEASE COME TO MY GARDEN PARTY
SUNDAY AT 2 O'CLOCK
TEA AND CAKES
PLANTS AND FLOWERS FOR SALE
EVERYONE WELCOME!

Quarrelsome Queen announced that she would be the guest of honour and would open the Garden Party. "You must have a Grand Opening Ceremony!" she told Golden Girl.

The day of the Garden Party dawned fine and sunny. Later, when everything was finally ready, Golden Girl opened the gates to her garden and was delighted to see all her Letterland friends waiting.

"I declare this Garden Party open!" shouted Quarrelsome Queen – but nobody was listening to her. They had all hurried over to the little table where Golden Girl was selling her plants and flowers.

"These are terrific!" said Ticking Tess, picking up a pot of tiny tulips. "They will brighten up my tower no end. I can put them on my telephone table."

"Look at this sunflower!" cried Naughty Nick. "I bet it will grow taller than me!"

By the time Quarrelsome Queen reached the table, she was at the back of the queue. She started to frown as the plants were sold, one by one. In no time at all, the table was empty!

"Don't worry, Your Majesty," cried Golden Girl. "I still have plenty in my greenhouse. I'll just run and fetch some for you." And she raced along the path to the greenhouse where she kept all the baby plants.

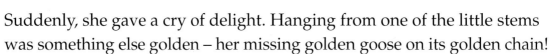

"What a good thing I planted these new ones the other day," she said to herself, as she reached for a pot of little golden roses.

Suddenly, she gave a cry of delight. Hanging from one of the little stems was something else golden – her missing golden goose on its golden chain!

"It must have fallen into the pot when I was planting the seedlings last week!" she exclaimed, fastening the chain very carefully around her neck again.

Golden Girl's Letterland friends were delighted to hear the good news, and they enjoyed the Garden Party even more.

Golden Girl gave everyone free tea and cakes, and she saved a special chocolate cake for Jumping Jim.

The Trouble with Telephones

by Jo Hallett and Julie McLaren

Ticking Tess woke up early one morning and yawned. "Time to get up," she said to herself, as she looked at the clock. "I mustn't be late for work!"

It only took two ticks for Tess to get dressed, then off she set to work at Teletouch Tower.

Her job is to keep everyone in Letterland in touch with each other by telephone. But this morning at Teletouch Tower something seemed different and she couldn't think what it was. That bothered her.

She went into her special room where she looks after all the machines that make the Letterland telephones work. Everything looked all right, but there was usually a gentle hum in the room with all the machines working, and now it was silent.

Ticking Tess rushed over to her control panel and picked up her own special telephone. She waited for the funny noise to tell her it was ready to be used. But there was only silence. That meant the whole telephone system must be broken! What could she do? Lots of people and animals would be wanting her to connect their telephone calls, and they would all be wondering what was wrong.

Tess ran across to the cupboard and grabbed her tool kit. She found a screwdriver and started to change some of the wires. Working quickly, she put a blue wire where an orange one had been, and a purple one where a yellow one had been. Then she turned a few knobs and pressed a few buttons and suddenly all the machines started buzzing and clicking, and gently humming again.

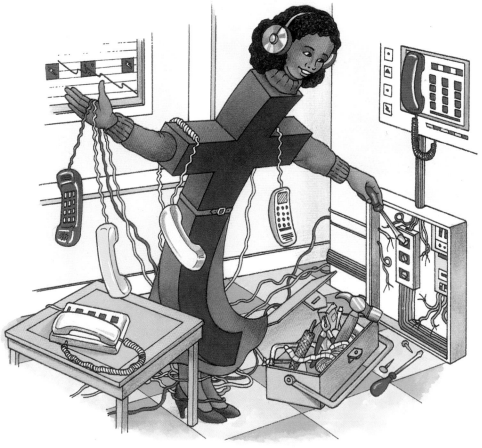

Ticking Tess felt very pleased with herself for fixing all the connections so quickly, so she decided to sit down and have a nice cup of tea. She thought she had earned it.

At about the same time, in the Letterland Castle, Kicking King wanted to make a telephone call. He picked up his telephone and listened for the special sound. When he heard it, he dialled the number.

4–1–5–2.

That was the number of the telephone in Hairy Hat Man's house.

"Hello! Jumping Jim speaking!" said a voice on the other end of the line.

"Jumping Jim?!" said Kicking King. "Oh, sorry – I wanted to talk to Hairy Hat Man!" He put the telephone down again and frowned.

A little later, Fireman Fred had a call from Naughty Nick who thought he was calling Golden Girl, and Sammy Snake had a call from Quarrelsome Queen who wanted to speak to Fireman Fred.

"Hello, Fireman Fred," she said. "I want you to come and check my electric fan to see if it's safe."

"I'm not Fireman Fred, I'm Sammy Snake!" said Sammy.

"Of course you're Fireman Fred," snapped Quarrelsome Queen. "I've dialled Fireman Fred's number, so you must be. Now come and look at my electric fan at once!" and she put the telephone down with a bang.

Sammy Snake didn't know what to do. He didn't know anything about electric fans and even he was sensible enough to know you must never touch electrical things. Still, he didn't want to make Quarrelsome Queen even more cross. She could be very frightening when she was in a really bad mood.

Then Sammy Snake saw Clever Cat through the window. She was talking to Kicking King.

"I don't understand," Clever Cat was saying. "You wanted to talk to Hairy Hat Man and you got Jumping Jim instead? There must be something wrong with the telephones. Let's go and talk to Ticking Tess."

Sammy Snake rushed after them. "Wait for me!" he called. "Quarrelsome Queen thinks I'm Fireman Fred, and she wants me to look at her electric fan. What shall I do?"

"Oh dear, more trouble with the telephones," sighed Clever Cat. "You'd better come with us. We're on our way to see Ticking Tess."

As they got near Ticking Tess's tower, they found a whole crowd of other Letterlanders on their way there too.

"Our telephones aren't working properly!" they all grumbled.

Even Quarrelsome Queen was among them. "It's quite preposterous!" she shouted. "I insist that the telephones be fixed this instant!"

Clever Cat pushed her way through the crowd to the Queen.

"Your Majesty," she said, very politely. "Ticking Tess needs help. If we all grumble and shout at her, we will only make it more difficult for her."

The door opened a little, and Ticking Tess's worried face peeped round. "Please come in, Clever Cat" she said in a small voice.

About ten minutes later, Clever Cat came out again, with Ticking Tess. "Please go home and try your telephones now," said Ticking Tess.

Everyone went home, and a few minutes later telephones could be heard ringing all over Letterland.

"Thank you, Clever Cat," said Ticking Tess, with a big smile. "I've learnt my lesson. Next time the telephones aren't working, I shall read my special book on fixing telephones before I try to mend them."

Now all the telephones are working well in Letterland, and Fireman Fred has fixed Quarrelsome Queen's electric fan, so everyone is happy.

Robber Red meets Santa Claus

by Vivien Stone

It was Christmas Eve and everyone in Letterland was busy wrapping presents. Everyone, that is, except Robber Red, who was busy stealing presents instead!

First, he had been to Ticking Tom's tall tower and taken the new telescope that Ticking Tom was going to give to Ticking Tess.

Then he had been to Kicking King's castle and taken the football that the king was going to give to the Letterland football team.

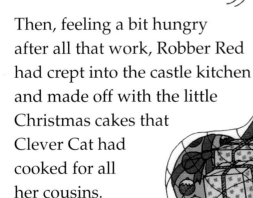

Then, feeling a bit hungry after all that work, Robber Red had crept into the castle kitchen and made off with the little Christmas cakes that Clever Cat had cooked for all her cousins.

Next, Robber Red had crawled into Bouncy Ben's burrow and had taken the bat and ball which Bouncy Ben had bought for his brothers.

Then Robber Red had hurried up to Munching Mike's home in the Mighty Mountains to see what he could find there. Munching Mike's Mum had some shiny new metal models to give to Munching Mike. Into the sack they went!

Last of all, Robber Red had hurried to Hairy Hat Man's house. There, he had stolen the special Christmas hats which Hairy Hat Man had made for the Christmas party he was having the next day.

When his sack was full to over-flowing, Robber Red had rushed home. It was just beginning to snow.

He breathed a sigh of relief as he reached his door. "Just in time!" he thought. "I don't want to leave footprints in the snow!"

He pushed open the door of his hide-out, and was just about to put his sack in his secret room when he saw someone fast asleep in his favourite armchair.

It was Santa!

Santa woke up with a start when he heard Robber Red.

"Oh, Robber Red, it's you! I was just having a little rest before I deliver my presents to Letterland," he said. "I've been working so hard that I feel worn out."

Then Santa noticed Robber Red's sack.

"Well, I must say, that's very kind of you, Robber Red. Thank you for bringing my sack in out of the snow," he said.

Santa stroked his beard thoughtfully for a moment.

"Robber Red," he said, at last. "I've a request to make. Would you mind delivering all these Letterland presents for me?" – and he waved his arm towards the sack. "I feel so tired tonight."

Robber Red blushed bright red with embarrassment.

"Oh . . . oh . . . all right," he stuttered, and he picked up the sack he'd been trying so hard to hide. Santa handed him his red coat with its warm hood and Robber Red went out and climbed on to the sleigh.

"The reindeer know where to go first," smiled Santa, and off they flew – straight to Ticking Tom's tall tower! So Robber Red felt obliged to return the telescope he'd taken!

Then the reindeer flew on to Kicking King's castle. And what do you think Robber Red had to give him . . . ?

Yes, the football! And then he ran down to the castle kitchen and replaced all the Christmas cakes.

By the end of Christmas Eve, the reindeer had taken Robber Red all over Letterland – and not only had Robber Red returned all the presents he had taken earlier, but he had delivered all of Santa's presents, too!

When Robber Red arrived back at his hide-out, Santa seemed to be feeling better.

"I don't think I will retire from this job after all," he laughed, "especially now I've got you to help me, Robber Red." Then, with a twinkle in his eye, he added, "You will help me again next year, won't you?"

When Santa had gone, Robber Red was suddenly struck by a dreadful thought. He was the only person in Letterland who had *not* received a present from Santa!

"Oh, I really must change my ways and not be such a rascal," he sighed.

Sadly, he went into his secret room to put away his empty sack – and what a surprise he had! There was a large, square, flat parcel for him on the table!

"Grrreat! Santa has remembered me after all," grinned Robber Red.

He grinned even more when he saw what was in the parcel. It was a book – but it had nothing written inside! And on the cover, in gold writing, were the words "Robber Red's New Year Resolutions!"

A New Job for Lucy

by Moira Andrew

Living in a lighthouse all by yourself can be a little bit lonely. Lucy Lamp Lady was lonely. She looked after the great light at the top of the lighthouse, which meant that she spent a lot of time alone. She longed to spend some time with other people for company.

She looked and looked all round Letterland, but the Letterlanders all seemed to be too busy to spend much time with her.

Hairy Hat Man was busy building a huge new house. "I'd like to keep you company, Lucy Lamp Lady," he said, "but I'm working hard on a new house for Humphrey the Hippo. Try Ticking Tess."

So Lucy Lamp Lady went off down Letterland Lane towards Teletouch Tower, where she knew she would find Ticking Tess. She took the lift to Tess's office and popped her head round the door. Ticking Tess was talking on her telephone as usual. When she had finished her call, Lucy said, "Hello, Ticking Tess, have you any spare time?"

"Spare time!" said Ticking Tess, tossing her hair. "Not in this job. I'm too busy keeping everyone in touch on the telephone lines."

"Lucky you," said Lucy Lamp Lady, and she walked off to ask someone else.

Next, she met Golden Girl. "Are you lonely?" she asked.

"No," said Golden Girl. "I'm too busy working in my garden and looking after my goats and my geese. If you're lonely, why not look for a job like mine?"

Now Lucy Lamp Lady wasn't lazy. She thought a job seemed like a good idea. So she left Golden Girl with her goats and geese, and went off to find Dippy Duck in her den by the duck pond.

"Do you need any jobs done, Dippy Duck?" she asked.

"No thank you, dear Lamp Lady," said Dippy Duck. "But I know that Fireman Fred has lost his lamp. He might have a job for you. You could light his way when he leaves the fire station to fight the fierce flames."

So Lucy Lamp Lady hurried on to the fire station as fast as her long legs would carry her. If there was a fire, he might need her help right away.

"Fireman Fred," she said. "I'm looking for a job. Do you need a lamp like mine to light up the fire engine for you?"

"I'd love to have light from your lamp, Lucy," said Fireman Fred. "But we must have a blue light on our fire engine and your lamp is yellow. I've sent a letter asking for a new lamp, and it will be here soon."

Lucy Lamp Lady felt more lonely than ever. "Nobody needs me," she sobbed. "No-one has time to keep me company and no-one will give me a job to do."

She didn't notice Max and Maxine, on their way home from the Letterland School. But they had heard Lucy crying. "We have an idea," they said. "Our lollipop lady has left, and there is no-one to lead us safely across the lane. Maybe you could be our new lollipop lady?"

Lucy's eyes lit up. "Yes, maybe I could learn to be a lollipop lady," she said. "And I'd love to be with all the little children! Thank you, Max and Maxine. I'll go along to the school today."

And that is just what Lucy did. The Letterland teachers were delighted, and they loaned her a lollipop sign while she learned all about the job.

"Look right, look left, look right again," said Lucy, as she led the little ones across the lane to the other side.

"Very good, Lucy," said the teachers. "You can have the job." They gave her a brand new lollipop sign and a lovely white coat.

Lucy felt very lucky. Now, she really had two jobs, one looking after the lighthouse to keep people safe at sea, and another keeping little children safe as they crossed the road.

So now every day Lucy leaves her lighthouse and takes her lollipop sign down the lane to the school. There, she looks right, looks left and looks right again, and then leads the children safely to the other side.

On foggy days, she smiles extra brightly, which makes her light shine right through the fog. All the cars stop and let the little ones cross safely.

Lucy Lamp Lady is so pleased with her new job that she has given Max and Maxine some large lemon lollies. "That's to say 'thank you'," she said.

Max and Maxine looked at Lucy in her lovely white coat. "Now you aren't just Lucy Lamp Lady!" they laughed. "You're Lucy Lollipop Lady as well!"

Naughty Nick's Good Day

by Katie Carr

As you might imagine, Naughty Nick finds it difficult to be good for very long. It isn't that he *means* to be naughty, but he just can't help playing tricks on other people. And if somebody tells him not to do something – well, he can't help trying it out just to see what will happen.

One day, for example, Naughty Nick went to visit his friend Zig Zag Zebra at the Letterland Zoo.

Zak the Zoo Keeper knew what Naughty Nick was like. "Whatever you do," he warned, "don't open any of the animals' cages. They might escape!"

Well, of course, when Naughty Nick heard that, he couldn't help opening one or two cages just to see whether Zak the Zoo Keeper was right.

First he opened the giraffe's cage and the giraffe galloped out of the zoo and started eating all the flowers in the hanging baskets and window boxes outside people's houses.

Then Naughty Nick opened the monkeys' cage and in no time at all there were monkeys scampering around all over Letterland. Some of them found their way into Hairy Hat Man's house and started trying on all his best hats.

The monkeys looked very funny, but as you can imagine Hairy Hat Man wasn't pleased *at all*.

Back at the Letterland Zoo, Naughty Nick was just about to let the lions out for a little walk, when Zak the Zoo Keeper noticed what he was doing and made him go straight home. His mother was very cross and sent him to bed early.

"I just don't know what to do," she sighed, when she went to tell Zak how sorry she was. "Nick isn't really a bad boy – he just doesn't think. If somebody tells him not to do something, he can't help doing it just to see what will happen. Whatever can we do to make him less thoughtless and more helpful?"

"I have an idea," said Clever Cat, who had been helping to find all the monkeys and return them to the zoo. "I think we can find a way to make Nick less naughty – at least for a little while."

She whispered something to Zak and Nick's Mum, and they both smiled.

The next day, Naughty Nick went back to the zoo, because it was one of his favourite places. He was surprised when Zak the Zoo Keeper smiled at him, but he was also very pleased that he wasn't going to be told off again.

He wandered over to the camels' yard to see what mischief he could get up to there.

"Oh, by the way," called Zak the Zoo Keeper, "please don't touch that brush in the corner of the yard. And whatever you do, you mustn't sweep the yard with it!"

Of course, as soon as Zak's back was turned, Naughty Nick picked up the brush.

"I wonder what will happen if I just sweep a little corner of the yard with it," he said to himself.

He swept a little bit of the yard, while the camels stood and watched him curiously. Nothing exciting happened, so Naughty Nick swept a little more of the yard. Still nothing happened.

So Naughty Nick swept the whole yard – and it took him a long time – but he couldn't see anything different when he was finished, except that the yard was beautifully clean.

Naughty Nick was feeling a bit tired by now, after all the sweeping.

"I'll go and have a little chat with Zig Zag Zebra, while I have a rest," he thought to himself.

So he wandered out again, being careful to shut the camels' gate behind him this time, and went to see Zig Zag Zebra.

"I'm just about to have my afternoon nap," yawned Zig Zag Zebra. "You can stay and have a nap too, if you like, but whatever you do, please don't put any water in those buckets over there."

Naughty Nick looked at the row of buckets standing by the water tap.

"I wonder why I mustn't put any water in them," he said to himself. "I'll just put a little drop of water in one of them and see what happens."

Can you guess what he did next? He filled every one of the buckets to see what would happen and, just as he was filling the last one, Zak the Zoo Keeper came along.

"Well thank you, Naughty Nick!" he said with a grin. "You've cleaned the camels' yard beautifully for me. I've never seen it look so smart! And now you've filled all these heavy water buckets for me, so I can take them to the animals. They need a drink when they're thirsty. You are a good boy!"

At first, Naughty Nick was amazed. He wasn't used to hearing people tell him he was a good boy – but then he decided that he rather liked it. Of course, he soon realised that Zak had played a clever trick on him, but he also decided that it was rather nice to be useful and to help other people.

So now, Nick helps Zak the Zoo Keeper every weekend, cleaning out the cages and feeding the animals. He always remembers to shut the doors and gates and he is much too busy working to think of naughty tricks to play. Well, most of the time, anyway!

Kicking King
and the Kittens

by Russ Smallwood

Kicking King had been looking after four little kittens, called Dandy, Lucky, Happy and Gus. Now that they were growing up, it was time to find them good homes. Kicking King thought that the kittens should only be kept by kind people.

On this particular morning in Letterland, Kicking King woke up late. Normally, the kittens squeaked as loudly as they could to wake him up so that he would make their breakfast. When he looked in their basket to see why they were quiet, Kicking King had a big shock. All of the kittens were gone!

Kicking King looked around the bedroom for the kittens. He checked under the bed and he looked in his cupboard. He even looked in the locker where he kept his football kit, but he couldn't find the kittens.

"Dandy! Lucky! Happy! Gus! Where are you? Please come back!" called Kicking King. But there was no sign of them.

"I wonder if they went to the kitchen to find their own breakfast," thought Kicking King to himself. "Yes, I think I should check the kitchen."

Down in the kitchen, Kicking King looked under the sink and under the table. He looked in the box where the cook kept kindling to light the fire. No kittens anywhere.

Just then he heard a little squeak coming from the cold store.

"The cook keeps the milk in the cold store," said Kicking King to himself. "They must have tried to get the milk." So he stood by a crack in the middle of the door, and listened. He called the kittens' names. "Dandy! Lucky! Happy! Gus!"

Yes, he could hear their squeaky voices. They must have gone into the cold store and the door locked behind them. He looked for the key, but it wasn't in the lock! "I must find the key quickly," he thought. "The kittens will get very, very cold. I think I need some help!"

Kicking King ran to
Hairy Hat Man's house.
When Hairy Hat Man
heard about the kittens,
he said, "Of course I'll
help you hunt for the
key. Let's hurry!
There's no time
to lose!"

As they were rushing back, they passed Dippy Duck and Lucy
Lamp Lady, who were having a picnic by the duck pond. "What's
happened?" they called – and when Kicking King explained, they
offered to help, too.

They ran past Golden Girl's garden. She looked up from her weeding
and called, "Goodness! Where are you three going in such a rush?"

Kicking King told her about the kittens and the missing key. "Poor
kittens!" she cried. "I'll help you. The more people there are, the better."

Back at Letterland Castle, Golden Girl looked all over the King's gardens for the key. Then she looked by the gate and on the grass, but still there was no key.

Dippy Duck looked in the dining room, then down by the drawbridge, but she didn't find the key either.

Kicking King stayed in the kitchen to be near the kittens. He wanted to talk to them through the crack in the door, to keep them company.

Lucy Lamp Lady looked in the library and the lounge, and in all the halls. No key. Finally, she shone her light into the darkest corners of the Castle, and even down the cracks between the floorboards.

"At last!" she shouted suddenly. "I can see the key! It's stuck down a really deep crack – but I can't reach it."

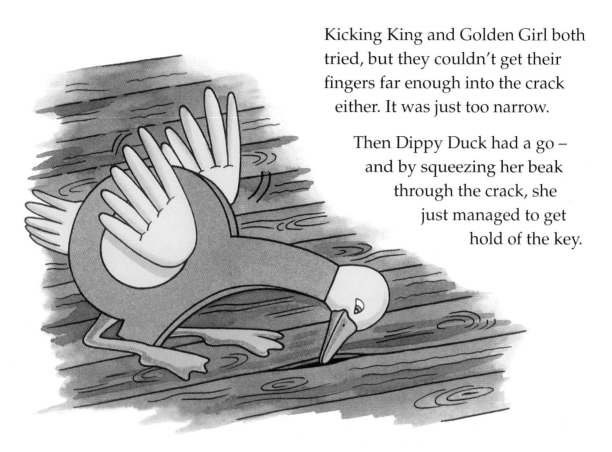

Kicking King and Golden Girl both tried, but they couldn't get their fingers far enough into the crack either. It was just too narrow.

Then Dippy Duck had a go – and by squeezing her beak through the crack, she just managed to get hold of the key.

"Hooray!" cried Kicking King, and he unlocked the door of the cold store as fast as he could . . .

CLUNK. CLICK.

. . . and out ran the four little kittens! They rushed straight into the arms of Kicking King.

"Well," said Kicking King, when he had finished stroking and cuddling the kittens. "I was looking for some kind people to give the kittens a new home, and I think I've just found them."

He asked his friends if they would like to have one kitten each, and his friends smiled happily at the idea. Lucy Lamp Lady chose Lucky, Hairy Hat Man chose Happy, Dippy Duck chose Dandy, and Golden Girl said she would love to look after Gus.

Then the moment came for the King to say goodbye to his kittens. He scooped them up one by one. Each one had a kingly kiss – kiss, kiss, kiss, kiss – and away they all went with their owners, each one to a lovely new home in Letterland.